WARRIOR
HEROES

MARCH

Bloomsbury Education
An imprint of Bloomsbury Publishing Plc

50 Bedford Square
London
WC1B 3DP
UK

1385 Broadway
New York
NY 10018
USA

www.bloomsbury.com

BLOOMSBURY and the Diana logo are trademarks of Bloomsbury Publishing Plc

First published in 2016 by Bloomsbury Education

A catalogue record for this book is available from the British Library.

ISBN
PB: 978-1-4729-2592-3
ePub: 978-1-4729-2593-0
ePDF: 978-1-4729-2594-7

2 4 6 8 10 9 7 5 3 1

Printed and bound by CPI Group (UK) Ltd, Croydon CR0 4YY

To find out more about our authors and books visit www.bloomsbury.com. Here you will find ex-
tracts, author interviews, details of forthcoming events and the option to sign up for our newsletters.

WARRIOR HEROES

THE SPARTAN'S MARCH

BENJAMIN HULME-CROSS

Illustrated by

Angelo Rinaldi

BLOOMSBURY EDUCATION
AN IMPRINT OF BLOOMSBURY
LONDON OXFORD NEW YORK NEW DELHI SYDNEY

CONTENTS

INTRODUCTION
THE HALL OF HEROES

The Hall of Heroes is a museum
all about warriors throughout
history. It's full of swords, bows
and arrows, helmets, boats, armour,
shields, spears, axes and just
about anything else that a warrior
might need. But this isn't just
another museum full of old stuff
in glass cases - it's also haunted
by the ghosts of the warriors whose
belongings are there.

Our great grandfather, Professor
Blade, set up the museum and when
he died he started haunting the
place too. He felt guilty about the
trapped ghost warriors and vowed he
would not rest in peace until all
the other ghosts were laid to rest
first. And that's where Arthur and
I come in…

On the night of the Professor's funeral Arthur and I broke into the museum - we knew it was wrong but we just couldn't help ourselves. And that's when we discovered something very weird. When we are touched by one of the ghost warriors we get transported to the time and place where the ghost lived and died. And we can't get back until we've fixed whatever it is that keeps the ghost from resting in peace. So we go from one mission to the next, recovering lost swords, avenging deaths, saving loved ones or doing whatever else the ghost warrior needs us to do.

Fortunately while the Professor was alive I wrote down everything he ever told us about these warriors in a book I call *Warrior Heroes* - so we do have some idea of what we're getting into each time - even if Arthur does still call me 'Finn the geek'. But we need more than a book to survive each adventure because wherever we go we're surrounded by war and battle and the fiercest fighters who ever lived, as you're about to find out!

CHAPTER 1

"The Spartans were more obsessed by war than any race, nation or tribe that ever walked the earth!" The Professor's ghost was pacing back and forth across the carpet in his study. Finn and Arthur knew they were supposed to sit and listen.

"They were the most feared warriors of the ancient world," he went on. "For hundreds of years they were the superpower of the Greek civilisation. But there was one thing, one battle, that defined the Spartans and their legacy. One moment that ensured their legend would live on for thousands of years. The battle of..."

The Professor paused and glanced at the boys.

"Thermopylae!" said Finn. Arthur rolled his eyes and sighed. He was used to Finn's memory for historical detail, but it still annoyed him.

"And that, my boys, is where you're going next!" said the Professor cheerfully.

"R-really?" Finn gulped. "Weren't the Spartans wiped out at Thermopylae?"

"Hang on!" Arthur joined in. "Are we talking about the battle where a few hundred Spartans were up against the entire Persian army?"

The Professor nodded and went on to give them

a few more details. The Persians were facing an army made up of a few thousand soldiers from the different Greek city-states, not just Sparta, he told them. But it was the Spartan king Leonidas who led this army and, when it was obvious they would lose, it was Leonidas and the Spartans who stayed behind and made a suicidal last stand.

"And I suppose that's how our next ghost died, is it?" Finn asked. "Killed by the Persians? But why would a Spartan warrior's ghost be unable to rest in peace after dying at Thermopylae? They dreamed of dying in battle, didn't they?"

"I didn't say our next friend was a Spartan," the Professor remarked cryptically. "In any case, it looks as though you're about to hear from the ghost himself."

Sure enough, the boys noticed that the

temperature in the room had dropped. The lights had dimmed. The pressure of the air in the room felt different too – a shift of some kind in the atmosphere. They heard slow steps in the hall outside, they saw the door handle turn, and both boys held their breath as they waited for the red-plumed, red-cloaked, bronze-clad Greek warrior of their imagination to appear. But the figure who entered was not what they had imagined.

True, he looked as solid as an oak tree and with his strong features and flashing dark eyes he must have been a fearsome sight on the battlefield. He wore no armour to speak of, though. His torso and upper thighs were protected a little by a tough-looking leather tunic, and his head by a leather helmet, but if the boys had hoped for a Greek hero, he did not look the part.

He looked from Finn to Arthur and back again, his face expressionless.

"So, you were at Thermopylae," the Professor began. "And what a great fight you and your people put up against the Persians."

"You speak of 'my people' as if I fought alongside my brothers, as if I fought to defend *my* people..." The huge ghost shook his head. "They said we would be remembered for all time... What fools we were. We fought. We died. We were forgotten."

"So, you're not a Spartan then?" Arthur inquired.

A look of pure hatred spread across the ghost's face. "My name is Adakios," he growled. "And I am a helot. A Spartan slave. The Spartans treated their dogs better than they treated my people. They came to my village, looking for fighters for

Thermopylae. They said my family would be made free. But while I was cut down fighting in their ranks, youths from the Crypteia were butchering my family in our home.

Sparta's secret police, that was how the Professor had once described the Crypteia – an elite force of young men whose job was to terrify the helots who worked the land around Sparta as slaves. As the last stage in their military training, the most promising young Spartan men joined the Crypteia, roaming the land in secret to spy on the helot slaves, uncover any plans they had for rebellion, and kill the bravest and best of them. In order to prevent the helots rebelling, Sparta officially declared war on the helots every year, so that it was never a crime to kill a helot.

It seemed pretty clear what it was that had caused Adakios's spirit so much torment.

"They promised immortality." His voice was a low groan now as he advanced towards the boys, arms outstretched. "And then they wiped out my family. Stop the Crypteia! Save my people!"

Before they could ask any further questions, Adakios had placed a hand on each boy's chest. The room seemed to fill with mist, the light grew fainter and fainter, the air grew warmer, and the boys' minds went completely blank.

CHAPTER 2

Arthur floated in darkness, his mind empty. Slowly, faraway sounds began to reach him. They grew louder, and Arthur realised he was listening to the cries and blows of battle. Something hard pressed against his back, and with a gasp he regained consciousness. The battle cries intensified but still Arthur could see only blackness. He tried to get to his feet but when his head cracked against hard rock he began to panic.

He twisted around, and for the first time he saw light. Silhouetted outlines of one man after another were inching forwards, each with a spear thrust ahead. *I must be in a cave!* he thought, and he started crawling towards the light. Gradually Arthur began to remember who he was, and where he had come from. He still couldn't remember the details of where he was now, but he knew he had to look for Finn.

As he drew nearer to the mouth of the cave he saw the shadowy figure of a soldier slumped against the wall. Instantly Arthur froze. The soldier was not moving, or making any sound. His head lolled at an ugly angle. *Must be dead*, thought Arthur. He stared hard at the shape of the soldier's head, waiting a little longer just in case. The man's helmet had a distinctive plume. *Ancient Greeks!* thought Arthur, and then the memories came flooding back. *Xerxes and the Spartans...*

He looked again to the mouth of the cave and caught his breath. No longer were the soldiers marching past. He could see the front lines of two armies clashing right in front of his eyes. On one side, festooned in gold and carrying large, wicker shields, Xerxes' men. On the other, under their proudly crested bronze helmets, red tunics fluttering, the Spartans! *This must be the front line of...* Arthur could hardly believe it but it had to be... *the Battle of Thermopylae!*

Heart thumping in the knowledge that he was caught up in a battle that would be remembered for thousands of years to come, Arthur wracked his brain for a plan that would get him safely out of the cave and off the battlefield. No scheme presented itself. The best he could come up with was to take the dead soldier's armour and weapons. He wasn't sure what he would do with them, but it was better than doing nothing.

Wrestling with the body's dead weight, Arthur unstrapped the armour and tugged off the soldier's red tunic. Then, piece by piece, he tried to dress himself in the bronze armour. The breastplate proved too big and cumbersome and he set it aside, but the greaves he buckled tightly to his legs, protecting his shins, and the helmet was not too loose on his head, although he was surprised at the weight of it.

Arthur had just picked up the Greek soldier's

sword and shield and drawn a deep breath when the front line outside the cave appeared to shift. With a roar, the Persians rushed forward as the Spartans fell back until none was visible at the cave mouth. All Arthur could see now was a crush of Persian soldiers, jostling against their comrades in front of them. His heart sank. He was all too aware that he was wearing Greek armour. All it would take would be one Persian soldier to look into the cave and Arthur would be as good as dead.

It was just at that moment that a low growl reached Arthur's ears, and with a sick feeling in his gut, he realised it had come from behind him in the cave! Arthur cried out in panic. He looked over his shoulder for the animal that had growled but saw nothing. He looked back to the cave mouth and saw that a Persian soldier had stepped into the cave and was staring right at him. Another roar went up from the soldiers outside as the Spartans were beaten further back. The Persian in the cave grinned wickedly at Arthur. Legs bent and sword drawn, the soldier walked carefully forward. Arthur stood transfixed, unsure what to do. Ahead, a vicious-looking human foe. Behind, who-knew-what in the cave.

Another growl propelled him into action. Hoping to catch the grinning Persian by surprise he sprang forwards, ran a few steps and lunged with his sword. The Persian sidestepped, letting Arthur past, slicing and missing as the boy turned to face him again. The Persian's smile broadened. He now had Arthur exactly where he wanted him – with his back to the Persian army at the cave mouth. Arthur feinted as if to strike with his sword arm, then punched the soldier with his heavy curved shield. But it was Arthur who was knocked off balance as the weight of the shield carried him forwards. The Persian drew his arm back ready to stab Arthur with the point of his sword. Arthur cringed and squeezed his eyes shut.

A deafening roar filled the cave and Arthur felt the Persian crash into him, sending them both sprawling to the ground. The air was all black eyes, white teeth, huge claws and the screams of the Persian as a bear tore into him. Arthur wriggled out of the way and recoiled, trying to press himself back into the wall of the cave. Too late he noticed that he had come up on the wrong side and the bear was in between him and the cave mouth. Barely able to think in his terror, Arthur began hammering his sword against his shield. The metallic sound rang out like the peal of a huge bell as he beat iron on bronze with all his strength.

The bear raised its head, blood dripping from its jaws. Arthur stepped forwards, hammering even harder. Bellowing with rage, the bear reared up, towering over Arthur and blocking out nearly all the light. Praying desperately that the noise he was making would be enough, Arthur stepped forward once more and almost collapsed with relief as the bear dropped down, turned and lumbered towards the cave mouth.

The bear's roar had caught the attention of the soldiers nearest the cave and they shouted in fear, unable to get out of the bear's path. It charged out of the cave and into the Persian force, scattering soldiers left and right.

A great shout went up as the Spartans seized this unexpected opportunity and bore down on the Persians, driving them backwards. Moments later red tunics and plumes replaced gold jewellery and wicker shields in Arthur's limited view. A Spartan stared in at Arthur and nodded, and he realised this was his chance to leave the cave. He took a deep breath, raised his sword, and walked out to join the Spartan ranks.

The men nearest the cave mouth gave Arthur a loud cheer as he stepped out. What had not been clear from inside the cave was that the Spartans were arranged in row after row of shield-wall formations. Each line of soldiers held their shields so that they overlapped with the next man's shield, creating a wall of metal. Arthur could not see how many rows of soldiers separated him from the front line, but judging by the noise it was not far away. In the course of his adventures Arthur had learned to use many weapons, and he was confident with spear and sword. But the close confines of pitched battle, where rows and rows of soldiers pressed up against one another, was a new and unwelcome experience.

"This is no place for a boy," someone shouted, echoing Arthur's thoughts exactly. "Get him to the back!"

To begin with Arthur thought that the soldiers had misheard the instruction, as they shepherded him away from the cave and sideways across their ranks rather than to the back of their lines. But he tripped and stumbled his way across, and seconds later he found himself standing knee-deep in the sea. He had assumed as he emerged from the cave that the battlefield was in a valley or gorge, but looking around him he saw that the fighting was taking place on a narrow strip of land with cliffs on one side and the sea on the other.

"Get back past the wall," a soldier instructed gruffly.

All Arthur had to do now was wade along the shoreline and he would soon reach relative safety. He winced as an arrow hissed into the water next to him, and he raised his shield over his head and began splashing through the small waves. Ahead he saw a low defensive wall of rocks extending across the land and a short way out into the sea. It seemed that the Spartans had come out from behind the wall to press the Persians back, and behind the wall Arthur saw a larger army of Greeks. He vaguely remembered the Professor talking about the different Greek units taking shifts at the front line. *Must be the Spartans' turn at the moment,* he thought as he reached the wall.

A strong arm reached down and pulled him up, and then he was slithering gratefully down the far side of the stone barrier.

EXTRACT FROM *WARRIOR HEROES*
BY FINN BLADE

THE BATTLE OF THERMOPYLAE

When the Persian emperor Xerxes prepared an army of over 100,000 troops for an invasion of Greece, more than half the Greek city-states immediately surrendered in the hope of peace. The city-states of Athens and Sparta led the resistance, and it was agreed that Sparta would lead a mixed Greek army north to try and stop the Persians getting very far into Greece. However, they decided that the Greek army would be made up of only around 7,000 men. They would be horribly outnumbered by their enemies.

Why? Partly because they wanted to keep most of their armies fresh to defend Athens and Sparta in the south. And partly because the Olympic Games were being held at the same time as Xerxes began his advance. As the Olympics were a hugely important religious festival, as well as a sporting spectacle, the Greeks wanted to allow their soldiers to attend the Games.

This small Greek army chose to wait for the Persians at the 'Hot Gates' of Thermopylae, a very narrow pass through which Xerxes' army would have to march if they wanted to reach southern Greece. On one side of the pass were sheer cliffs. On the other side was the sea. Because the battlefield was so narrow, it didn't really matter that the Persians outnumbered the Greeks so heavily.

After two and a half days of fighting, in which the Greeks didn't give an inch, they were betrayed by a local villager, who told the Persians about a goat track that they could take to get around the pass. Leonidas, the Spartan king who commanded the whole Greek army, heard that the Persians were going to outflank the Greeks, and immediately told most of the army to retreat. The Spartans who stayed behind were all killed along with Leonidas, but they fought for long enough to allow the rest of the army to escape.

CHAPTER 3

Some way behind the defensive wall, Finn woke with a stretch. He blinked up at the sky and cleared his throat. The word 'Sparta' floated around his head. *Maybe I'm in Sparta,* he thought calmly. Somewhere close by, Finn could hear men shouting but he felt too sleepy to care. *Maybe if I just close my eyes...* he thought, yawning deeply. A scuffling sound made him turn his head. Before he could react, flying sand filled his mouth and a young man crashed into him. The youth had been running fast and his momentum sent him flying high over a spluttering Finn, who was now very much awake!

Finn's first instinct was to get away. The last thing he wanted was to draw attention to himself before he found Arthur and got his thoughts together. But as he and the young man both scrambled to their feet, the look on the youth's face made him stop. His nostrils were flared, his throat seemed tight, and his eyes were wide with terror.

"Help me!" said the youth. "Find Adakios! Tell him Nikodemos needs him. Please!" But before Finn could reply, the young man had turned on his heel and darted behind a large boulder and out of sight. It occurred to Finn that this was a great piece of luck – here was a ready-made reason for Adakios to listen to him. He also realised that whoever the youth had been running from was probably not someone he wanted to meet.

Too late.

"You there!" a man called. "Did you see the slave?"

Finn looked up to a truly intimidating sight. A young man loomed over him, a look of savage hatred twisting his face into a grotesque mask. His long, dark hair fell about his shoulders and he wore the red tunic of the Spartans. In one hand he carried a long whip, and in the other he held his sword in a tight, angry grip that made the veins in his forearm stand out.

"Did you see the slave?" the young Spartan shouted. "Tell me now!"

Finn swallowed and shook his head.

"If I find you have lied, boy..." the Spartan began. But then a shout went up.

"We have him, Drakon!"

Finn was almost relieved, until he saw the pitiful state of Nikodemos as two other young soldiers dragged him, whimpering, across the dust and threw him at Drakon's feet. Part of Finn wanted to creep away, but somehow he could not tear himself from the scene.

"Do you imagine that you helots are safe from me just because we are at war with Xerxes?" Drakon addressed the trembling youth.

Nikodemos shook his head, not daring to look

up at his tormentor.

"With whom is Sparta always at war, slave?" Drakon asked, slowly drawing his sword.

"With the helots, master," the youth replied.

Finn felt his stomach turn. He had a near-perfect memory for everything the Professor had taught him, and it had saved his life many times before. The word that came to the forefront of his thoughts as he saw the young Spartan towering over the slave in the dust was 'Crypteia.' Wasn't it the Crypteia who had massacred Adakios's family and neighbours?

This isn't right, thought Finn. *He's going to kill him.*

"Please, master!" Nikodemos begged. "I have done nothing wrong. I am here to serve the army. I want to do my part."

Drakon's upper lip curled back in a sneer.

"Do you know how we in the Crypteia serve Sparta?" he snarled, raising his sword over his head. "We do it by killing helots!"

"No!" Finn blurted out, unable to stop himself. "Surely we need every man alive. Xerxes outnumbers us by thousands!"

Drakon's head whipped around and his eyes flashed pure fury at Finn, who instantly regretted his intervention. How was this helping with their mission? All he was doing was getting himself into trouble. It was usually Arthur who messed everything up before they had even started.

"The boy is right, by Zeus!" a voice boomed out. "This is not the day to kill those who help us fight, Drakon, although the fighting is now over for today. We have held the pass for another twenty-four hours and brought glory on Sparta.

It was Spartans who pushed forward beyond the wall today and Spartans who drove the Persians back to the east gates of the pass. But still, we need our men alive! What crime has this helot committed?" The voice belonged to a huge Spartan soldier who brushed past Finn, ignoring him, and advanced on Drakon.

"Since when did a Spartan need a reason to kill a helot, Aristodamus?" Drakon retorted. As soon as the words had left his lips the colour drained from his face. "Sir, I didn't mean to question..." he spluttered. His excuses turned to a yelp as the older man's fist connected with his jaw and he rocked back on his heels. Drakon's two companions shrank back as the soldier loomed over their fallen friend and growled at him.

"Your arrogance weakens you, Drakon, and

it weakens Sparta. Report to me later for a whipping. First we must all attend the sacrifice to Ares and pray that he brings us victory." With that Aristodamus strode away. Finn's eyes followed the big man, and he saw now that he was on the outskirts of a camp. *Must be where Arthur is too,* Finn thought, and he was about to investigate when he heard Drakon's snarl. The beaten young Spartan made no attempt to conceal the malice he felt towards Nikodemos.

"I'll send you to Hades, pig," he hissed. "I'll come hunting for you, and when I've finished with you, I'll come hunting for your family. Now run!"

Nikodemos darted away without a backward glance, and Finn too made a hasty departure towards the centre of the camp before Drakon could redirect his anger at him.

After quite a search, Finn caught sight of Arthur sitting next to some Spartan soldiers, and approached them cautiously. He was used to having to rescue his hot-headed brother from whatever crisis he had managed to create on arrival, but this time it appeared that Arthur was not in any trouble at all. In fact, as Finn approached, one of the soldiers slapped Arthur on the back and the rest of the group cheered and laughed. Finn caught something about a bear, and then Arthur glanced up and saw him. At once Arthur made his excuses and got up to join his brother.

They wandered over to sit in the dust under a small, gnarled tree, and shared their experiences so far.

"Bears, Persians, Spartans – it's hard to know who to be most scared of!" said Arthur.

"Actually, I think it's the Spartans we should be most worried about," said Finn. "I know we're sort of on their side at the moment, but don't forget it's them who killed Adakios's family." Finn reminded his brother of the sinister Crypteia, and of their habit of killing helots just to show them who was boss.

"When I was in the battle I could see which soldiers were Spartans and which were helots," Arthur remarked. "The helots have much more basic armour and helmets. But they were treated the same as the Spartans by the leaders. Not like slaves at all."

"Well they're fighting the same enemy right now I suppose. But I saw how Drakon looked at

Nikodemos today. And let's not forget that the problem for Adakios is saving his family from the Spartans."

The brothers' conversation turned to Adakios and how to find him. Finn suggested that they wait for a while and see whether it just became obvious, but as usual Arthur wanted to take a more direct approach.

"It will be fine," said Arthur, brushing aside Finn's objections. "They think I brought good luck because of what happened with the bear. I can ask a few questions without them wanting to kill me. Anyway, we should stick together. If Drakon wants to take his frustration out on anyone it'll be you, so standing next to the army's good luck charm won't do you any harm!"

The same thought had been at the back of Finn's mind. He had no intention of getting caught alone by Drakon, and though he would rather they keep completely out of the way, Finn went along with Arthur's suggestions.

The soldiers looked at Arthur with fatherly kindness as he made his enquiries, and nobody paid any attention to Finn. After a few minutes they found a soldier who knew a fighting helot called Adakios, and he directed them towards a barrel-chested man who was sitting on a rock a short way off. The helot glanced up as they approached and both boys recognised him immediately from their first meeting in the Professor's study.

"It's about Nikodemos," said Finn before Arthur could say anything. "We have a message for you." Adakios stared hard at Finn, and then rose to his feet.

"Let's walk," he said, and led them through the camp before scrambling a short way up a steep scree slope and settling on another rock. He stared again at Finn. "Tell me," he said.

Finn described what had occurred earlier with Drakon and Nikodemos. He took care to emphasise Drakon's threat to Nikodemos's family. In his moment of need, Nikodemos had wanted Finn to ask Adakios for help, and Finn was hoping that the two helots were either related or at least from the same village. At first he thought he'd made a mistake. Adakios's face betrayed no emotion whatsoever as he listened to Finn, and he sat in silence for a long while after Finn had finished talking.

"You do realise," Finn began again, "that it's not just Nikodemos who is in danger, it's..."

"It's every man, woman and child cursed to have been born within reach of Sparta!" Adakios growled. "Nikodemos is my nephew and we live on the same farm. If Drakon plans to find Nikodemos's family then he's a threat to me, my wife, my son – everyone! And they promised land for my family in return for my fighting!" He fell silent again, brooding on these grim new circumstances.

"We should leave tonight," said Arthur.

"Shut your mouth, boy!" Adakios hissed. "Say that within earshot of a Spartan and you'll be dead before your next breath! They don't take kindly to deserters. And there is no 'we'... I'll be going alone."

"But we came to you because Nikodemos asked for your help," said Finn. "And now we need your help too."

"When they find you've gone they'll want to know what I said to make you leave," Arthur chimed in. "Lots of them know I was looking for you."

"And Drakon wants me dead too," said Finn. "Don't forget he'll blame me for his whipping..."

Adakios shook his head and sighed, but the boys could see that he felt he had no choice.

"Tonight then," said Adakios. "We'll wait for the sacrifice to begin. Everyone should be distracted."

EXTRACT FROM *WARRIOR HEROES*
BY FINN BLADE

BECOMING A SPARTAN WARRIOR

Sparta was the only city-state in Greece to have a professional army. In fact nearly every feature of Spartan society was designed to make its army more effective. To be a true Spartan man was to be a Spartan warrior, and to be a Spartan woman was to marry and give birth to Spartan warriors.

At birth, babies were examined by an elder. Legend has it that those who showed signs of weakness or defects were thrown off a cliff, as they would not grow into strong warriors or women who could produce them.

THE AGOGE

Formal military training began at the age of seven, when boys began a training programme known as the Agoge and stopped living with their parents. The Agoge was designed to create tough warriors who were loyal to Sparta. The process of making them tough involved harsh treatment like limiting them to one new item of clothing per year and deliberately underfeeding them so that they developed the cunning and stealth to be able to steal food. Stealing like this was actively encouraged, but anyone who was caught was severely beaten. The idea was to learn to steal without getting caught.

THE CRYPTEIA

At the age of eighteen, boys became reserve soldiers. At the same time the most promising young warriors became part of the Crypteia, a sort of secret police made up of trainee warriors. The sole purpose of the Crypteia was to terrorise the helots (Spartan slaves). This achieved two Spartan goals. Firstly it taught the young warriors to spy, to hunt and to kill. Secondly it kept the helots frightened and less likely to rebel against Sparta.

CHAPTER 4

With a little questioning, carefully undertaken to avoid displaying their ignorance, the boys learned that the sacrifice would take place at nightfall. Although fighting had stopped for the day, a contingent of soldiers was left defending the wall in the pass in case the Persians should decide to mount a night attack. The rest of the Spartan army was gathered in camp.

Following Adakios's lead, the boys did their best to avoid eye contact with anyone else, hoping to attract as little attention as possible. From time to time one soldier or another would slap Arthur on the back and make a comment about the bear, but by and large they were left alone.

The light was just beginning to fade when Adakios touched each boy on the shoulder and motioned with his head. They had agreed that as sunset approached they would make their way to the outskirts of the camp, but just as they began to move there was a shout.

"Over there – he's with another boy!"

With a feeling like snakes writhing in his stomach Finn recognised Drakon's voice and moments later the cruel youth blocked their path. Standing behind him was Aristodamus, the huge Spartan soldier who had intervened earlier.

"What were you planning with that helot who ran away, boy?" Drakon shouted.

He's trying to save his skin, thought Finn, and it looked like it might be working. The soldier behind Drakon was staring hard at him, and Finn remembered what the Professor had said about Spartans being constantly paranoid about helot rebellions.

"Master," Adakios cut in, "these boys are here to serve..." he trailed off as the soldier raised his hand, palm out, to silence him. The huge man had shifted his gaze to Arthur.

"You, boy," he said. "It was you who drove the bear from the cave today, wasn't it?" Arthur nodded and Aristodamus chuckled. "King Leonidas has heard of your bravery and commands you to stand with him as we make our evening sacrifice to Ares. The bear was a good omen!"

Finn's blood ran cold when he saw the glare Drakon shot his way, and it did not go unnoticed by Adakios either. Worse still, Arthur was then led away by Aristodamus and there was nothing anyone could do about it. They would have to wait for Arthur to find an opportunity to slip away, only now he would have to escape the attention of King Leonidas himself!

"Is that King Leonidas?" Finn asked and Adakios nodded. For all the danger they were in, Finn couldn't suppress a small pang of envy that Arthur was getting to meet the great Spartan leader.

"Soldiers!" King Leonidas called, and instantly

the men fell silent. "Today, by your strength and the will of Ares, Xerxes and his Immortals were resisted!" A loud cheer went up at this.

"By the courage of this boy here," the king went on, putting a hand on Arthur's shoulder, "by the rage of the bear he drove out into the Persian ranks and by the might of every man here, the Persians will not overcome these lands." The cheering grew louder.

"And by this sacrifice we pray that Ares fights with us again tomorrow." The cheering stopped abruptly as a tethered goat was led forward and handed to the priest. Leonidas prowled around inside the circle of fire, his face full of passion, and began a prayer to his god as the priest lifted the goat up onto the altar.

"Oh great Ares, God of War," Leonidas's voice

boomed out across the camp. "Chariot-rider, strongest of all, fearsome with the spear, saviour of cities and destroyer of the weak..." The priest began muttering an incantation and preparing the goat for sacrifice, sprinkling wine on the animal's head and drawing a gold-handled dagger from his cloak. Finn was so transfixed that he only barely registered that Arthur was slipping out of the circle.

"Rule our hearts again tomorrow, oh great Lord of Armies," Leonidas continued. "Lead us once more. Put strength in our arms and bellies. Fight with us as we do battle. Lift us up that we may honour you, and crush all fear as surely as you crush Xerxes and the Persian horde."

The priest raised his knife aloft for a brief moment before it flashed down and killed the goat in a moment. The crowd remained totally silent as the priest turned the dead goat belly up and sliced it open, revealing the inner organs. One by one he removed them and held them up to inspect in the firelight. Nobody moved. At length the priest gave a signal to King Leonidas, who raised his arms aloft.

"The omens are good, the gods are with us, and Ares has heard our prayer!" A roar went through the crowd as if the soldiers were already celebrating victory and a sort of frenzy took hold as the men began leaping and dancing.

Moments later Arthur appeared in front of Finn and Adakios, and without speaking the three of them began to proceed through the camp. Adakios led them to a tent on the outskirts and sat them down outside it. He handed round some goat's cheese and figs, and a water skin.

"Not too much," he instructed. "We have a long night ahead and we will have to move fast!" He looked pale and anxious, the thought of a vengeful Drakon and his comrades in the Crypteia clearly causing him much alarm.

"Drakon's no match for you, surely!" Finn wanted to reassure Adakios, but the big man shook his head.

"Don't you know what the Crypteia are capable of?" he said hoarsely, handing a dagger to each boy. "And Drakon's been shamed. When he says he will hunt Nikodemos down he means it. And when he says he'll go after the family next he means that too. It happened in a village near us when I was a boy. When the Crypteia make you a target, you run away or you die, and I'm not going to let my family die."

"So, where will we run to?" asked Finn.

"Athens," said Adakios immediately. "Athens and Sparta are fighting together against Xerxes for now, but we all know they are enemies at heart. I've heard of other helots who have escaped to Athens. I think they welcome us there just to anger the Spartans. Here, take these." He passed a bow and a quiver of arrows to each boy, and they settled into a nervous silence. Finn was glad of the bow and arrows though – the bow was his weapon of choice and he was an excellent marksman.

A soldier carrying a flaming torch and a whip strode by with a younger man following. When they were just a few metres away the youth turned his head to stare right at him, and

Finn drew in his breath sharply. It was Drakon. The youth took in the scene, looked long and hard at Adakios as well as the brothers, stared at their weapons, and without making a sound he grinned and drew his finger across his throat.

"You see," said Adakios when they were out of earshot. "We have to go now and take whatever head start we can get!" They got to their feet, tucked daggers into belts and slung bows across shoulders, and began to slip away from the Greek camp just as the first crack of a whip hitting flesh reached their ears. They took no pleasure in hearing their enemy's punishment. It was obvious to all of them that the lashing would serve only to make Drakon hate them even more.

Silent and alert, they picked their careful way

along the rocky path that hugged the shoreline and led away from the camp. Ahead they could see torchlight and Adakios motioned to the boys to follow him off the track. They pressed themselves into gaps between rocks as the torchbearer approached. It was a solitary Spartan soldier and Adakios slipped his dagger from his belt and tensed, then watched as the soldier walked past, oblivious to the three fugitives.

Adakios set off again at a pace that was somewhere between a slow jog and a fast walk, and the boys soon settled into his rhythm. They had only been going for a few minutes when Adakios came to an abrupt halt. The boys saw his raised hand's shadow in the darkness and stopped as well, hearts thumping with the tension. Someone ahead was whistling.

We're far enough from the camp now that it's obvious we're running away, Finn thought, shivering silently as he considered what the Spartans were likely to do with deserters.

All of a sudden Adakios chuckled, and then began whistling himself. Moments later a shadowy figure appeared in front of Adakios and embraced him.

"It's Nikodemos," Adakios said quietly.

"I didn't know what else to do, Uncle," said Nikodemos. "So I just waited for you." He cast a nervous glance at Finn and Arthur.

"You did well," said Adakios, and Finn and Arthur introduced themselves. Nikodemos relaxed when he recognised Finn.

"Did Drakon get his whipping?" he asked.

"He did," said Adakios. "And he will be hot

on our heels soon enough. We must press on quickly. He won't travel far tonight after his punishment, but in the morning he'll be after us. We need to cover as much ground as we can and find somewhere to..." he trailed off mid-sentence. "Well we can talk about that later," he concluded. "For now, let's move!"

CHAPTER 5

All through the night Adakios kept up the same efficient pace he had set from the beginning. The moon appeared and disappeared. The boys' minds became so numb with tiredness that they barely noticed their surroundings and when dawn's first light began chasing the shadows away they were shocked to find themselves on a mountain path.

Finn gazed around at the ridges and valleys and was about to speak when he lost his footing and crumpled to the ground with a shout. Arthur reached down to help his brother, and Finn winced as he stood, an angry scrape across his calf slowly beginning to well up with blood. He took a few steps, limping heavily, and sank to the ground once more.

"OK, we rest." Adakios nodded curtly. "But we should get off the path."

He led the way, scrambling, towards an overhanging crag that loomed high above them. They crossed under it, then climbed up over it, and eventually came to rest sitting on top of it in the shade of a second crag. From here they could see a good distance back along the path but would be all but invisible to those below.

"I'll keep watch," said Adakios. "The rest of you, sleep."

Nikodemos and the boys slumped gratefully down, and sleep found them almost immediately.

The sun was high in the sky when Adakios shook the boys awake. They both stretched and rubbed their sore limbs, stiffened by sleeping on hard rock.

"Our turn to keep watch?" Arthur mumbled sleepily. Adakios shook his head.

"Nikodemos and I traded places a few hours ago. We have all rested now. We continue."

Finn groaned and rubbed his leg. Regardless of the monstrous purple bruise on his calf, the thought of more walking, on legs more tired than they had ever been, was too much to bear.

"Come on, boy, you said you wanted to come

with me," Adakios barked. "Sore legs or death at the hands of the Crypteia – which do you prefer?" Finn groaned again and urged his legs forward, his bruised calf throbbing in protest, and soon they were speed-trudging along at the same pace Adakios had forced through the night.

"It's past noon," said Adakios over his shoulder. We'll stop at sunset or when we find a good place for an ambush – whichever comes first."

"An ambush?" Arthur queried. "I thought we were running from the Crypteia, not trying to trap them!"

"We are running," said Adakios grimly. "But believe me, Drakon will be running faster..."

All through the previous night they had been so tired that Drakon seemed a distant threat, and it was unnerving to be reminded of what and who they were up against. Two boys and two helots against a group of well-trained Spartan warrior-psychopaths who were out for revenge... It was a sobering thought, and it propelled them all forward with renewed energy.

The afternoon ticked slowly by, each minute lasting an age as aching legs and bursting lungs screamed their objections. Water skins were refilled in the streams they passed, but the only incident of note was a chance encounter with a goatherd who was driving his flock along the trail in the opposite direction. He hailed the exhausted band of travellers and asked where they were heading.

"To Olympia, to watch the Games," said Adakios without missing a beat. But as he spoke this lie, Finn thought he saw something cross

Adakios's face. It was a new fear, a new realisation of some kind. Finn stored the observation away. There would be time for questions later...

The goatherd's eyes widened. "Olympia!" he gasped. "Fare well, you have far to travel!"

Finn and Arthur exchanged a glance, the same question in each of their minds: *just how far do we have to travel?* It hadn't occurred to either of them to ask when they set off, but they had no idea how far Sparta was from Thermopylae, or how long it would take to walk there. Arthur tried to ask Nikodemos when they had resumed the journey, but the young man had no sensible answer, and Adakios was already too far ahead to hear the question, or so it seemed.

Afternoon was just turning to evening when the path led them through a narrow passage between two slabs of rock. Emerging on the other side of this passage, the path crossed a stream and wound through more of the huge boulders that the boys were getting so used to. As a place to mount an ambush, it could not have been more obvious.

"Drakon will be on his guard when he comes through that passage," said Adakios, looking up at the reddening sky. "But we are out of time. We stop here."

Finn and Arthur could have wept with relief, and Nikodemos looked close to tears of exhaustion too. They sat down to rest for a while, and eat and drink a little. Adakios was looking around, taking in their surroundings. He asked the boys to demonstrate their aim with the bow and arrow, and seemed pleased enough when each hit a thin sapling some distance away at their first attempt. Next he darted off to clamber up and around the rocks so that he was peering down into the passage from above, and then he did the same thing from the other side.

Rejoining the others he explained again that they simply would not be able to outrun Drakon and his friends if they were following.

"They will catch up," he said, "so we might as well choose where that happens! Anyway, we don't have to beat them outright – we just have to slow them down..." He explained that he would position two of them as snipers ready to shoot back at the mouth of the passage from sensible vantage points, and that the other two would take up positions atop the rocks on either side of the passage, from where they would be able to shoot down on the Crypteia once they realised they could not go forwards. Knowing that they could be waiting all through the night or maybe longer, they decided that one person would keep watch from up on top of the rocks, and the rest would wait together a short way off the path, ready to take up their positions as soon as a signal was given by the lookout.

They each familiarised themselves with the positions, and with the detail of the terrain around them as far as possible, and then Nikodemos took up first watch as the light began to fade.

"How far to Sparta?" Arthur asked at length.

"Still four days to go," Adakios replied.

"Four days!" Finn breathed. "Would he really be able to track us across that sort of distance if we just kept going?"

"Maybe not, but I need to know he's behind us and not in front of us heading for my wife and my farm. Better still if we can kill him. But even then his comrades would come for us. We have to get home before they do, and then there's Argos..."

"Who's that?" Arthur asked.

Argos, it turned out, was Adakios's son. Some time ago, Adakios told them, Argos had been taken on as a servant to a Spartan family who were currently attending the Olympic Games.

"So when you said we were going to the Games at Olympia..."

"It was a lie. We have to get to the farm. Argos is safe."

"But if you get away to Athens he'll never know where you went..."

Adakios rubbed his temples, a look of agony on his face, and nodded miserably.

"Get some sleep," he whispered. The conversation was clearly over, and the boys did as they were told, but both were wondering the same thing. If Adakios escaped without his son, would his spirit really be appeased in the future, or would he be haunted by regret at having left the boy behind?

Arthur slipped into a fitful sleep, but Finn could not, despite the tiredness in his body. He lay gazing up at the emerging stars, wondering how they were going to get through this adventure. As he mulled their situation over, he began to feel that they would have to find a way of bringing Adakios's son Argos with them. What the soldier's ghost had wanted was to save his family. Leaving his son behind with a Spartan family, to face who-knew-what fate when they discovered what Adakios had done, simply wouldn't cut it. He turned and looked at Adakios.

"Tell me about Argos," he said.

"He's a good young man," said Adakios, sighing and rolling onto his back. "Strong. About Drakon's age. And he's clever. He'll know how to survive."

"How can you be so sure?"

"I have to be sure. What choice is there?" Adakios barked. His raised voice woke Arthur, who opened his eyes and listened quietly. Finn waited a few moments.

"There might be a way we can bring Argos," he said at length. Then, when Adakios did not reply, he went on. "Arthur and I could go to Olympia and get word to him, while you go back to the farm. Then we can arrange to meet somewhere..."

He left the thought hanging in the air, and for a while Adakios did not respond. Then he sighed.

"It is a brave thing that you offer to do, Finn," he said in a tired voice. "But you're boys. I cannot send you on such a dangerous journey alone."

"Hold on," said Arthur indignantly. "In case you've forgotten, King Leonidas made a point of telling everyone how brave..." But the sentence trailed off. From somewhere back down the path came the sound of barking dogs.

All three sprang to their feet and grasped for their weapons, Adakios whispering urgent instructions as they did so.

"Finn, to the rock opposite Nikodemos. Arthur, you shoot from here. I'll cross the stream."

Finn began picking his way back down to the path.

"Good luck, mate," his brother whispered after him. He had his bow and quiver slung across his back, and using both hands for balance, careful not to dislodge any rocks, he was soon back on the trail. The dogs sounded much closer now, and he was not sure of his ability to reach the top of the rocks above the passage before the dogs got to him. *They have to be Drakon's dogs,* he thought, feeling slightly sick with nerves.

He crossed the stream and began to scramble up the rocks just as the first dog sprinted out of the passage, barking furiously. In panic, Finn tripped, and then the barking stopped with the hiss of an arrow and a yelp, and he heard the dog limping away.

"Cerberus!" The cry came from some distance away but there was no mistaking Drakon's voice.

The barking stopped entirely. However many other dogs there were, they had been called off and the Crypteia knew they were near their quarry. Any element of surprise was over.

Finn hauled himself to the top of the rocks and took up his position, waving silently at Nikodemos. He strung the bow, set his quiver down next to him, nocked an arrow, and waited...

CHAPTER 6

The drone of crickets throbbed in the warm night air, and Finn's heart thudded in his ears like a war drum. A bright moon shone down on the empty path. The Crypteia had seemingly melted into the night with their dogs. Finn strained with all his senses for some indication of their attackers' whereabouts, but to no avail. *They know we're here and all we've done is scare off a dog*

– not much of an ambush! Finn thought as the wait continued. He shifted his weight from foot to foot, tensing and relaxing the muscles in his legs to stop them becoming stiff. *Where are they?*

He stopped to check he knew exactly where his quiver was and as he did so an arrow hissed over his head. He dropped to the floor to the sound of Drakon's laughter.

"You think you can outsmart the Crypteia?" the Spartan jeered. Finn was nearing blind panic. Drakon's voice was close, somewhere near the base of the rocks before the narrow passage. There was still no sign of the other Spartans Adakios had warned would be with Drakon. Perhaps he came alone, Finn hoped, and then he felt a shiver course through his body as he heard the scraping sound of a stone being dislodged.

It had come from the rocks on his side of the path. Someone was climbing up from the path on Drakon's side of the passage.

Of course! Finn thought. They weren't stupid. They knew they'd be killed if they tried to make it through the passage, so they were trying to climb around it. Finn suddenly felt extremely vulnerable. Although he could see the path from his vantage point, he could not see the rocks that an attacker would climb to reach him. The whole plan had relied on catching the Crypteia by surprise. Now that they knew where he was, he was an easy target, and someone was coming for him!

He cast around for a safer place to lie in wait. If he could just find somewhere unexpected and regain the element of surprise...

He slid back from the top edge of the passage and crawled towards the edge of his platform. He would not be visible to anyone on the path, or on the other side of the path now. He inched forward, hoping to catch a glimpse of whoever was climbing up the rocks, but his view was blocked by a slightly lower shelf of rock. He slipped down onto it and crawled forward again, peering over the lip.

His breath caught in his throat. Staring up at him from no more than six metres below was a red-cloaked Spartan with a long dagger in his teeth, and the Spartan was climbing towards him. Finn recoiled out of sight and tried to re-nock his arrow, his hands trembling as he heard the Spartan scrambling rapidly upwards. Holding his breath, Finn rolled to the edge of

the rock once more and pushed himself up to a kneeling position to take aim at the Spartan, who was now on less steep ground and had let go of the rock with one hand and was holding his dagger back over his shoulder, ready to throw it. The arrow and the dagger were released at the same moment. Finn and the Spartan were so close together – separated by less than three metres now – that their projectiles collided in mid air and neither found its mark.

In a heartbeat Finn realised that he had left his quiver on top of the rocks. He snatched at the dagger in his waistband, just as the Spartan, grinning, drew a vicious-looking sword that flashed in the moonlight. Worse still, Finn could now see that another Spartan was climbing up behind the first.

All of this had happened so quickly that Finn hadn't had time to think about Nikodemos and the others, but he thought of them now and shouted out to Nikodemos for help. He glanced over and saw that Nikodemos was not above him any longer. Finn shook in terror. The Spartan closest to him was still grinning, and was stepping carefully towards him, crouching, ready to spring. Finn held his dagger out in front of him in both trembling hands, and the Spartan just laughed. Then Finn lost his nerve entirely, and turned to run. He bounded back up to the top of the rocks, not looking for a better vantage point now but simply running away. He had the presence of mind to snatch up his quiver as he passed it, and then he heard the Spartan shout in pain. He risked a glance over his shoulder and was just in time to see his attacker clutching at an arrow in his throat, toppling backwards and disappearing to the sound of more shouting.

Finn scanned the rocks on the other side of the passage again, searching frantically for Nikodemos. There he was! Nestled in a crevice that meant he would not be visible to Drakon or anyone else climbing up from that side, Nikodemos had found the perfect sniper's position from which to cover Finn's side of the passage. Suddenly Finn understood what was needed. He had to find his own position and protect Nikodemos, just as Nikodemos was protecting him. He raced back to the lower ledge from where he had first shot at the Spartan and peered over the edge. The man with the arrow in his throat lay motionless in the dust below, while the second Spartan, who had clearly been knocked back down the rocks by his falling friend, was dragging himself back along the path and away from the passage. Judging by the fact that he seemed barely able to crawl, Finn guessed that both his legs must have been broken in the fall.

He looked back to Nikodemos and raised an arm in thanks. But as Nikodemos nodded his acknowledgement, Finn felt that sick feeling of dread again. Traversing around the rock towards Nikodemos's crevice was another red-cloaked assailant, and it looked to Finn as though it was Drakon. He shouted out a warning. Nikodemos couldn't see Drakon, but he understood Finn's warning and started to climb up and out of the crevice, back towards the top of the rocks. Finn snatched for an arrow and sent it hissing across at Drakon. But the Spartan was moving quickly and the arrow narrowly missed him, flying under his arm and clattering against rock. Drakon redoubled his efforts and skittered across the rock face like a monkey before leaping up the way Nikodemos had gone, and suddenly both men were out of sight.

Finn's stomach turned as he heard cries of pain, and then a roar from Drakon.

"It is as I said, helot," came Drakon's triumphant bellow. "And next it will be your family!" He appeared again at the edge of the rocks on his side of the passage and stared across at Finn, fists clenched, arms outstretched.

"Your family!" he roared again. Finn shot another arrow, and again Drakon moved out of harm's way. Just as it began to seem to Finn that Drakon was invincible, the Spartan snarled in surprise and pain as an arrow came from somewhere below and lodged in his arm. He clutched at it and disappeared from view, and moments later Finn could hear Drakon scrambling back down the rocks.

Adakios was scrambling up towards where Nikodemos must be lying as Finn watched for another opportunity to shoot at Drakon, but the Spartan was alert to the danger. He was protected by the rocks as he descended, and then stayed well off the path so that he could beat a swift retreat without being seen.

Adakios bounded up the last of the rocks

towards Nikodemos, while Finn and Arthur stayed in their positions. Finn knew in his heart of hearts that Nikodemos must be dead, but he still found a lump rising in his throat as Adakios reappeared, slowly carrying a limp and motionless body down towards the path.

As dawn broke the following morning, Adakios was still awake. He had instructed Finn and Arthur to try and rest, and despite everything sheer exhaustion had driven them both swiftly to sleep. Through the night Adakios had made a grave for Nikodemos out of small rocks, and in the darkness he had prayed for his nephew's safe passage in the afterlife.

By the time he shook the boys awake, Adakios had stripped the fallen Spartan of his food supplies, refilled the water skins, extinguished the fire and was ready to resume the march. His face, normally expressionless, was drawn tight with worry.

"Get up!" he ordered as the boys rubbed their aches. "We have no time. Now we've killed at least one of the Crypteia, as soon as Drakon finds another Spartan we'll have a small army on our tail. Either that or he's waiting half a mile back, ready to catch us unawares later on..." His face was pale, and the boys did as they were told, acutely aware that Adakios had just buried his nephew.

They dragged themselves to their feet and prepared for another day's march. Wordlessly, Adakios struck up his aggressive pace once again, and the boys were soon lagging well behind. They agreed that they needed to persuade Adakios to let them go to Olympia and find Argos while he returned to his farm. There was no other way that they could be sure he would feel everything possible had been done to save his family. They would need to bide their time though, and they settled in for another long walk, waiting for the right moment to present itself.

In the end, it was Adakios himself who brought the subject up. They were resting in the shade during the heat of midday when he spoke for the first time since they had set off that morning.

"If we escape to Athens and leave Argos with his master Theras, he will die. That is certain. Whether it is Drakon, or someone else in the Crypteia, Sparta will make an example of him to deter other helots from running."

The boys said nothing.

"And if I do not return to my farm directly, Drakon may well get there before me and I cannot bear the thought of what he will do to the rest of my family if he does. My wife, my brother, his remaining sons – I have to get to them before Drakon."

"If you give us directions to Olympia…" Arthur suggested once again. Adakios held up his hand and nodded.

"You are right. I don't know where you came from. Maybe the soldiers spoke true. Maybe you did bring the army good luck. You certainly helped Nikodemos, so who am I to refuse your help? You will find Argos and he will bring you to our farm."

Adakios explained that they still had two days' walk to complete together before their paths would diverge for one final day, the boys heading to Olympia, and Adakios to his farm near Sparta. The challenge they all faced was immense – to outwit the Crypteia and escape from Sparta - but the boys both felt something had changed. The challenge was clearer now, even if the enemy remained hidden. They both felt that if they could reunite Argos with Adakios, and see the family on their way to possible freedom, then they would have accomplished what they were there to do.

EXTRACT FROM *WARRIOR HEROES* BY FINN BLADE

KINGS, WARRIORS AND SLAVES

Spartan society was ordered in a very strict way.

• At the top were the kings. There were two kings at any one time so that each could make sure the other conducted himself properly and in the interests of Sparta.

• Next were the full Spartan citizens, the Spartiates. To become a full Spartan citizen as a man you had to complete your military training in the Agoge and then be accepted into a military unit as a full warrior. With very few exceptions, you also needed to be

Spartan by blood - related to the families who lived in and around the city of Sparta.

• Then there were the perioeci. These were free men who were not Spartan by blood, were not warriors, and were not full citizens. As the Spartan warriors were not allowed to engage in business for profit, the perioeci were the ones who made and traded goods.

• Finally there were the helots. They were slaves, although they had better lives than many slaves. They were mostly farmers who worked land and gave a high percentage of what they grew to the Spartan state to feed its warriors. The helots were the conquered people from lands surrounding Sparta. Because there were so many more helots than Spartans, the Spartans were always on their guard against rebellions.

Although the Spartans were very proud of their status as the finest warriors in Greece, that did not mean they didn't allow helots or perioeci to fight in the army. In fact often they forced them to. At the Battle of Thermopylae, Sparta contributed 1200 men to the Greek army. Only 300 were full Spartan warriors - the rest were helots or perioeci.

CHAPTER 7

Three days later, Finn's nerves were frayed. He couldn't escape the fear that Drakon or his Crypteia comrades could catch up with them at any point, and since they and Adakios had parted that morning, both boys had been feeling extremely vulnerable. The anxiety intensified as the road grew busier, for as they neared Olympia they encountered more and more people travelling in both directions.

"Drakon won't have any problem killing us in public, you know," said Finn. "He's a Spartan and we're helots as far as he knows."

Arthur stopped in his tracks and grabbed his brother by the shoulders.

"Stop worrying about Drakon," he snapped. "Even if he is following us, he'll want to see where we end up – to find out where Adakios and Nikodemos come from." He lowered his voice as a few people stopped in the road and stared at the boys. "We have to focus on the Olympic Games now. If we don't leave here with Argos, the whole mission will be a failure. Then what?"

Finn's brow creased. They had never failed to give a ghost from the museum what he or she needed to rest in peace. And it was only when the ghost was laid to rest that the boys were brought back to the present in the Professor's study. They had always wondered what would happen if they failed. Would they be stuck in the past forever? They had seen many times and places on their adventures, and some of them would have been quite exciting places to get stuck and live their lives. But the idea of being stuck as Spartan slaves was horrific, and Finn shuddered. He fingered the carved stone charm that Adakios had given him to help prove to Argos that the boys carried word from his father.

"You're right," Finn said. "Let's talk it through."

The boys went back over what Adakios had told them. They knew that Argos would be at the Games to serve his master, Theras, who was due to compete in the pankration.

"Do we even know what that is?" Arthur asked.

"The pankration is the toughest event at the Games," said Finn, recalling a long conversation with the Professor on the subject. "It's like a cross between wrestling and kickboxing. Basically it just means fighting without weapons. You can do pretty much whatever you want to your opponent."

Arthur snorted. "Sounds just right for these Spartans!"

Finn agreed. Everything they had seen of the Spartans so far confirmed the legends. They were totally fixated on fighting and war. They were ruthless and cold and cruel. You could admire their commitment but there seemed to be little or nothing to love about them, and brutal hand-to-hand fighting seemed like the event Spartan boys would dream about!

The brothers decided that when they arrived at Olympia the first thing they would do was ask around for information about Theras and the pankration. Hopefully they would be able to find Argos quickly and could be on their way. From time to time on the road they would see a red Spartan cloak, and each time they did they would think of the fighting at Thermopylae, and of the grave danger they were in, helping helots to escape the most feared warriors in history.

Such was the tension that neither boy had really thought about the fact that they were heading for the birthplace of the Olympic Games, and it was only as a bend in the road brought the buildings of Olympia into view that they began to feel more excited than afraid. They could see several buildings that looked like temples with their round columns. In fact almost every building seemed to be a temple. This was obviously a place just for the Games, not for normal life. There was nothing that looked anything like a stadium, but in the distance there seemed to be a large crowd of people standing on a wide grassy bank. As if on cue, the crowd started cheering at something the boys could not see.

"I guess that's the stadium then," Arthur remarked. Finn nodded.

Ahead of them, the road approaching the temples was lined with market stalls. The shouts of the vendors and the sweet smells of the food they sold mixed to create a sense of normal human warmth and the boys soaked it up gratefully after the hardships and hostility they had faced.

"Shame we don't have any money!" said Arthur, chewing on a piece of the dried meat they had acquired earlier in the journey. They had collected figs and olives as they walked, and had swapped them for other food whenever they found the opportunity.

"Well maybe someone wants some figs," said Finn hopefully. "And anyway, it gives us a reason to talk to people and find out when the pankration is going to take place. Let's split up and meet over there where the stalls stop. We'll take one side of the road each."

They divided the figs between them and made their way slowly from stall to stall, offering figs as payment for anything that took their fancy and asking as many questions about the Games as they could get away with. By the time they met up again just outside the temple complex they knew a lot more, even if they had not managed to find many people willing to accept figs in exchange for other goods.

Finn broke out some sweet bread he had acquired and the boys shared what they had learned. The competitors in the pankration would make their sacrifices to the gods later that day. They would sleep in a building called the Leonidaion, near the temples, without any family members or servants, before taking part in the main event the following day.

"So if we can find Argos and persuade him to leave tonight," Finn mused, "there's a good chance that his master won't even know about it for twenty-four hours..."

"Lucky we got here today!" said Arthur.

"We just need to find out exactly when and where the pankration competitors will make their sacrifices and then we should be able to figure out which one is Theras. Then we follow him to..." The words died on Arthur's lips and he gulped as a red-cloaked Spartan strode towards them. Both boys were on their feet immediately and were about to run when the Spartan called out to someone behind them, waved, and marched past without turning his head. It was a timely reminder of the dangers that awaited them, and the boys finished their conversation in whispers.

They agreed to split up again. As Finn made his way back to the market stalls in search of more details about the pankration and the sacrifices, Arthur took a more direct approach. He headed into the temple complex and, seeing a gang of boys hanging around near a large, plain-looking building, he wandered over to them.

"Can you tell me where the Leonidaion is?" he asked. The boys stared at him and laughed.

"It's right there," said the tallest of them eventually, pointing at the wall behind him.

"Alexios!" joked another. "Do you think he's here to enter the pankration?" The others doubled over at this, pointing at Arthur and howling with laughter. Never one to disguise his anger, Arthur reddened. The boy who was mocking him was bigger than Arthur, but not by much, and Arthur, unable to restrain himself, began to square up for a fight.

"Relax, my friend, relax," said the taller boy, Alexios. "We mean no harm. Nobody in their right mind would enter the pankration!

It's vicious and it's mostly Spartans who go in for it, and we're not Spartans..." Alexios faltered. "You're not a Spartan are you?" he asked. Arthur shook his head.

"Thanks to Zeus!" Alexios replied. "Anyway, what do you want with the Leonidaion? They won't let you in, you know."

Arthur explained, with some bending of the truth, that he was looking for a friend who served a Spartan wrestler.

"Theras?" Alexios repeated the name as soon as he heard it. "I've seen him, yes. He went off to watch the chariot racing at the hippodrome earlier. And he's easy enough to recognise. He's young but he has completely white hair. Why don't you go and have a look? Maybe your friend Argos is there now."

Arthur shook his head. "I need to find my brother first, but thanks." Alexios shrugged, and Arthur headed back to the market. A few minutes later he found Finn chatting to a date seller. Finn extracted himself from the conversation and Arthur filled him in. They soon agreed to head straight for the chariot races and try to locate Theras. Jogging back towards the temple complex, the boys were facing the direction of the crowd up on the bank they had noticed earlier. Arthur saw Alexios and his friends, still hanging around outside the Leonidaion, and was about to wave when he saw something that chilled his heart. He grabbed Finn's arm.

The gang was talking to a red-cloaked Spartan. He appeared to drop a few coins into Alexios's hand. Immediately the boy pointed towards the market. The Spartan turned to reveal a bandaged arm. There could be no mistake. It was Drakon!

Arthur dragged Finn across the dusty open ground towards a temple and ducked around one of its corners.

Both boys were on the edge of panic. They had assumed Drakon would pursue Adakios to his village and the sight of him so close by had been a nasty shock.

"His dogs must have been following our scent, not Adakios's," said Finn. "And now he's paid those kids, they'll be spying for him." A long silence followed.

"We still have to find Argos," said Arthur eventually. "If we don't, Adakios will never be at peace."

"Yes, but if those boys have told Drakon who

we're looking for," said Finn between short, panicky breaths, "we're finished. He'll know exactly where to find us."

"Relax, my friend, we haven't told him who you're looking for." Finn and Arthur spun around, unsure whether to fight or run. Alexios had come around the other side of the temple and approached them from behind.

"I don't like Spartans," he went on. "And he definitely doesn't like you two. I told him to go and look in the market, that was all."

"How do we know we can trust you?" Arthur hissed.

"Well if I wanted him to find you, I'd have told him where to look! You think I didn't see you coming back? Anyway," he said, shrugging, "if you can't trust me you're finished, like you said.

But if you do trust me I can help. I've sent the boys out to look for your friend, Argos. They're smart boys and it won't take them long, and as soon as they find him they're going to bring him to one end of the hippodrome. Follow me there and you'll see your friend soon enough."

Arthur and Finn both knew that Alexios was right. They had no choice but to trust him, and they agreed to follow him to the appointed meeting place, which appeared to be where the crowd they had seen was gathered. It was a nervous walk, both boys glancing around furtively no matter how hard they tried to appear casual. They felt a little better as they gained the cover of a jostling crowd and made their way along one edge of the hippodrome. They could see nothing beyond the next few bodies as they followed their guide through the crowd, making slow progress until the ground sloped down and the crowd began to thin out. A roar went up and the boys were treated to brief glimpses of chariots, each pulled by four horses, flashing by with their charioteers standing on platforms mere centimetres above the ground. It looked like a desperately dangerous circus act, but the boys were too tense to enjoy it. They stood, and waited, and sweated, Finn clutching at the carved stone charm Adakios had entrusted to them.

EXTRACT FROM *WARRIOR HEROES*
BY FINN BLADE

THE OLYMPIC GAMES

The Olympic Games were first held in 776BC. People would come from all over the Greek world to watch and take part. The Games were held every four years, and in order to take part, competitors had to swear that they had trained for at least ten months to make themselves worthy.

The Games weren't just about sport. They were also part of an important festival in honour of the god Zeus.

The Games were also a chance for rival Greek city-states such as Athens and Sparta to put their differences aside for a while and come together. Even during times of war, the enemies would observe a truce while the Games took place so that warriors could attend the festival and honour Zeus.

OLYMPIC HIGHLIGHTS

• Pankration: This was an anything-goes unarmed fighting event with two rules: no biting and no gouging. Everything else was allowed. You could kick, punch, headbutt, elbow, pull, twist and generally break your opponent until one of you gave in.

• Chariot racing: A single racer would stand in a small cart with an open back, drawn by two or four horses depending on the race. They would race several laps of a racetrack called a hippodrome. Although not legally allowed to crash into their rivals deliberately, in practice this happened a lot, leading to lots of crashes and making for a very dramatic event!

• Sprint: Just as it is now, the sprint was the most prestigious event. Runners would sprint one length of the stadium, which was around 190 metres, from a standing start.

CHAPTER 8

When Argos arrived, it was just as Adakios had said it would be. Finn showed him the stone charm and Argos believed them instantly. The brothers thanked Alexios and explained they had much to discuss with Argos. Alexios took the hint quickly enough, and wandered off with his friends while Argos led the boys away from the hippodrome and then on, away from the temple complex in the opposite direction to the market. They entered a camping field and passed through it until they reached a wooded area beyond. Here Argos gestured for the boys to sit in the shade and offered around a water skin.

Finn studied Argos as they caught their breath. The family resemblance to Adakios was striking. They shared very strong features, jet-black hair and large, flashing brown eyes. Most of all, however, Argos had the same sort of serious, dignified manner as his father: quiet, reserved, but seemingly ready for just about anything.

Just as well, thought Finn as he began the tale that Argos needed to hear. The helot's face betrayed only the faintest signs of emotion as the predicament was explained, his nostrils flaring slightly at the news that Drakon had sworn revenge on the whole family, and his eyes burning when Finn told of Nikodemos's death. He sat in silence for some time after Finn had finished, staring at the ground.

"And you boys," he said eventually, "why have you done so much for my father and me?"

"Drakon is after us too," said Finn quickly, praying that his answer would be enough. "We thought we had a better chance with your father on our side..."

Argos sat in silence a while longer and the boys waited anxiously, all too aware that Argos could still decide he wanted nothing to do with them.

"You're right about that," he said eventually. "We'll leave at dusk." The boys' shoulders slumped with relief.

"Now listen," Argos said briskly. "Here is what you must do..."

* * *

"Here we go again then," muttered Finn as he and Arthur shared some bread and dried meat. Just as they had at Thermopylae, the boys found themselves hiding beyond the fringes of the settlement at Olympia, ready to escape the Spartans. Argos had told them to go ahead and wait for him to join them after sunset when his departure would be less obvious. The brothers had split up in the hope that they would be less obvious to Drakon's roaming eyes, and those of anyone who accompanied him, and they had reunited beyond the market stalls at the bend in the road where they had first caught sight of Olympia that very morning.

It was there that they waited for Argos, hidden a short way back from the roadside as they had agreed. The wait gave them time to discuss what lay ahead, which was just as well now that the situation had changed so dramatically.

On the one hand it was good news that Drakon was not slashing and burning his way through Adakios's farm. This meant that they would probably find Adakios at home rather than on the road to Athens, which made life a little easier. On the other hand they had to assume that Drakon would pick up their scent again soon and come after them, and it would not take him long to realise where they were heading. At that point it would become even more of a sprint, for there was a good chance that Drakon would hear about Argos running away and put two and two together. Then his case for punishing the helots would be much stronger and he might well persuade a group of Spartans to join him in suppressing what he could say was a helot rebellion.

It was therefore with great excitement that the boys greeted Argos when he appeared leading three horses!

"Whose are they?" Arthur asked.

"They belong to Theras and his family," Argos replied. "It makes no difference taking them, or the food in the saddle bags. As soon as he discovers I have run away he will come after me. Mount up!" He waved the boys over to the horses and they were delighted to obey. The thought of another two or three days tramping on foot across southern Greece had not been sitting easily with either of them.

Sitting astride a horse was far preferable

and they set off at an eager trot into the night,
leaving Olympia and the Games behind them.

* * *

Finn jerked awake and a low moan escaped his lips as a twig snapped nearby. In his nightmare he had been running, naked and alone, through a pine forest with a pack of ravenous wolves in hot pursuit. They matched his running speed so they were permanently one bound away from sinking their stinking teeth into the back of his neck. He rubbed his eyes and tried to shake off the feeling that he was being watched by an unseen predator. In the grey dawn light, he could see no sign of danger through the thin trees in any direction. Argos and Arthur slept nearby, next to the horses and beneath the blankets they had used as saddles. With a twinge of guilt, Finn remembered that he was supposed to be keeping watch. The feeling of eyes on his back refused to go away, and he crawled over to the others and shook them awake.

"What is it?" said Argos, instantly alert.

"There's someone out there watching us," Finn replied. "I can feel it."

Argos sprang to his feet. "We should get moving – come on."

They roused and untied the horses and moments later they had resumed their journey, trotting through the woods and out onto a wide, open plain as light from the rising sun began to warm the air and ease their nerves. *Not that Drakon would have any problem killing us in broad daylight,* thought Finn, but he kept the thought to himself.

Argos told them that they should reach the farm before nightfall, and this thought perked everyone up. It felt as though they had covered more ground in the previous five days than in the whole of the rest of their lives. What was more, the thought that they might soon reunite with Adakios was a great comfort.

Throughout the morning they encountered little by way of traffic on the road towards Sparta, but as the sun reached its full height in the middle of the day and the heat forced them to pause and find shade, they saw a small group of exhausted-looking soldiers trudging towards them. They were clearly helots, protected as Adakios had been by leather armour not bronze, and although Argos and the boys would sooner have been left alone, the men came and rested with them in the shade by the side of the road.

"Are you returning from battle? Thermopylae?" Argos enquired.

"Xerxes is coming," one man replied bluntly. "We fought for three days. A few thousand of us against a hundred times that many of the Persians. But Leonidas chose the battlefield well. The pass at Thermopylae is narrow and we were holding them back."

Arthur was looking away all through the conversation. As soon as the soldier had confirmed he and his comrades were returning from Thermopylae, Arthur had realised there was a danger he would be recognised.

"So what went wrong?" Argos asked.

"Someone must have betrayed us and shown the Persians a way over the mountains so they could outflank us," the man replied. "Leonidas and the Spartans stayed behind. The rest of us retreated and now, thanks to Zeus, we are returning to our homes."

The conversation moved on to the question of how Xerxes and his army would treat the people of southern Greece when he marched to Athens. There seemed to be little belief, or hope even, that the Persians would be merciful, particularly when it came to Athens, the heart of Greece.

All through the afternoon they heard the same nervous warning: Xerxes is coming. The more they heard it, the more desperate they grew to see Adakios, for if Xerxes and the Persians were advancing on Athens, then their planned escape route simply led from one death to another.

CHAPTER 9

The sun was beginning to sink into the horizon as Argos, Finn and Arthur stood knee-deep in a fast-flowing river. They were close now, Argos told them as they washed and drank. The farm lay less than an hour away downstream.

"We will arrive after nightfall," said Argos quietly. "That is good – we do not know what we will find when we get there."

Finn had been thinking the same thing. Drakon had not been seen since Olympia and they assumed he was behind them. But it was possible he had overtaken them if he had acquired a horse of his own, or worse, sent word to others in the Crypteia.

"Adakios might not even be there!" said Arthur. "What if he's already left for Athens?"

"My father will know that is not a good plan by now," said Argos. "But if he has gone he will leave us a sign of some kind, I am sure. Come, it will be dark by the time we find out."

So they mounted their horses for the final part of the journey. Somewhere in the distance a dog barked, then stopped abruptly. Little else besides the horses' hooves and the droning of cicadas disturbed the dusky peace, and none of them felt like talking.

The first stars were piercing the night sky by the time Argos, who was up front, brought them to a halt. They climbed down, following the youth's lead silently, and tied the horses to a tree by the river. Proceeding on foot, they followed a path that hugged the riverbank and took them away from the main road. They could see a clutch of small houses up ahead. All seemed to be well. Firelight could be glimpsed through gaps in walls, and the sound of muffled conversation escaped with it.

Argos barely slowed, all thoughts of caution forgotten now that he could see his home, and Finn turned to Arthur. But Arthur was nowhere to be seen. Finn was about to call out to his brother when a hand clamped roughly over his mouth and a huge arm pinned his own arms to his chest and hoisted him off the ground. Feet bicycling wildly in the air, Finn was dragged off the path and into the bushes. He sank his teeth into the hand over his mouth, and received a bone-crushing squeeze across the chest in reward. Blinking back tears, Finn started to panic. How had they been so stupid? They knew the Crypteia might be waiting for them and they had walked straight into a trap anyway!

Somewhere close by, Argos cried out in alarm, and then in anger, "It's me, you fool! And where are the two boys? They're my friends." To his great relief Finn was set back on his feet and he turned to give his former captor a pained stare. The man smiled a little and motioned Finn back to the path, where Argos was standing with a small group of strangers.

"I'm sorry, Argos," one of them was saying. "But if you are with the boys then you will have heard what happened to Nikodemos and your father. We are watching for the Crypteia."

"Is Adakios harmed?" said Argos shakily as Arthur emerged with another man and took his place next to Finn.

"No, no, he is well enough, though he will be better now that you are here. Let's go to him."

"Who's here?" came a familiar voice, and then Adakios was with them, hugging his son long and hard and clapping Finn and Arthur on the backs. Argos began to talk of Thermopylae and Xerxes, but Adakios told him to wait, and led them all inside one of the houses.

The boys slumped gratefully down onto the floor cushions, while Argos's mother hugged her son and refused to let him go.

"Release me, Mother!" said Argos, laughing. "You should meet our guests."

Adakios introduced his wife, Kassandra, who tearfully thanked each of them for helping to reunite the family. Next the men who had ambushed them were introduced as Nikodemos's father and brothers. The father, in particular, wore a haunted expression.

"Drakon!" said Finn, reminded of the danger they faced from the Crypteia. "He followed us, Adakios, not you. And he will have followed us here if his dogs have our scent."

Nikodemos's brothers muttered dark threats, but their father silenced them. "Justice means nothing to the Spartans!" he snapped. "If one of the Crypteia has sworn us dead, then he will soon have his wish if we stay to face him. And if you kill him? How many other helots will the Crypteia kill in retribution? Adakios is right – we have no choice but to run."

"All the same," said Adakios, "perhaps you and my nephews could go back and watch the path once more, in case Drakon is close by." The younger men were only too happy to take up their watch again in the hope that they might have the chance to take revenge on Drakon, and they left the house immediately.

Meanwhile Kassandra handed out bowls of rabbit stew. It was the first hot food that the boys had eaten since their arrival at Thermopylae, and it was enormously comforting. As they ate, Argos relayed the warnings they had heard from the soldiers on the road.

"Athens may not be the best place for us, Father," said Argos.

Adakios nodded slowly. "I was doubting the plan in any case. It's another long journey, and there'll be plenty of Spartans between here and there."

"How close are we to Sparta now?" Finn asked, and then nearly choked on his stew when Adakios told him that the city was less than twenty miles upstream. What if Drakon had followed them as far as the river and then turned towards Sparta to find comrades from the Crypteia? They could track them to the farm and launch an attack at almost any moment!

"The danger will still be great," Adakios was saying, "but our best course may be to take the boats downstream to Gytheum, and then take our chances on the open sea and try for the biggest of the islands. The sea's twenty miles in the other direction," he clarified, nodding at Finn.

"Father, all we have are two river rafts..." said Argos, round-eyed.

"People have crossed the seas on rafts before," said Adakios. "It's that or we try and evade the Crypteia as a group of ten people from here to Athens..."

Argos nodded, though Finn and Arthur remained unsettled by his initial reaction. Their thoughts were interrupted by the sudden noise of an animal screaming, soon joined by others.

"The horses!" cried Argos. "Something has spooked them. We must hurry!" Everyone leapt into action. Kassandra grabbed some bags that were waiting by the door. Argos and Adakios snatched up their weapons.

"Argos!" his father barked from the doorway. "Get everyone to the rafts! I'll fetch your cousins."

"With me!" Argos cried, putting an arm around his mother and leading her through the door. As Finn and Arthur followed they heard the screams of the horses intensify, accompanied, not far enough away, by the barking of dogs.

"It must be Drakon!" cried Arthur breathlessly as they scurried after Argos. They dashed the short distance from the houses to the river and onto a rickety wooden jetty, Argos guiding his mother onto the larger of the two rafts and waving the boys onto the other. Finn followed Argos's example and untied the raft he and Arthur were on before looping the rope around one of the jetty's legs so that they were still moored, but ready to cast off in an instant.

Nikodemos's brothers came running towards them, and Finn waved them onto Argos's raft. He and Arthur were there to help Adakios look after his family, Finn reasoned.

"Go!" he shouted. "We'll wait for your father." Argos did not hesitate. He shoved off from the jetty, lifted the steering pole high in the air and then thrust it down into the water, propelling the raft out into the middle of the river where it caught the current and accelerated away silently into the night.

Moments later Adakios was with them on the jetty.

"They're too close!" he hissed. "They'll know we went downstream and they'll catch us unless we leave the raft here to throw them off."

Finn was about to protest but the look in

Adakios's eye made him think better of it. He quickly retied the raft.

"The horses are upstream," said Arthur. Adakios nodded and slipped into the river. The boys did the same, gasping as they adjusted to the temperature. Then, holding onto the roots and rocks that projected from the riverbank, for the boys at least were chest-deep in the water and it was moving fast, they pulled themselves quietly forwards against the direction of the current. In a moment they had rounded a boulder and were out of sight of the jetty. Already they could hear shouts, barks and the crashing sounds of the houses being ransacked. Soon they noticed the smell of smoke and moments later the night sky was lit up by the blaze of a thatched roof going up in roaring flames.

They made their way in grim silence along the bank until they reached the spot where the horses were tethered. They had calmed down now that the dogs had passed them by, and as Adakios and the boys stepped out of the river to see the horses alive and well, it seemed for a moment that they just might be able to escape the Crypteia.

"Just where have you crawled out from, helot?" someone asked in a loud, gruff voice. Standing on the path, a short way back from the horses, was a group of around ten men. Not young men these, and not from the Crypteia: they were fully fledged Spartan soldiers.

"And what's burning up that way?" one of them demanded.

"Masters," said Adakios respectfully, "I am just

returned from Thermopylae. And that up ahead is my farmstead being burned to the ground by Drakon of the Crypteia."

All of a sudden the sound of barking, which had been there in the background all along, grew louder and closer, until two wolf-like canines sprinted around a bend in the path and came to a snarling stop in front of Finn, backing him up against a tree. They were unmistakably similar to the dog they had injured back in the mountains.

"Looks like it was you they could smell all along!" said Arthur, smirking at Finn despite the danger.

Finn wasn't listening. He was too busy staring at the man who had been hunting them all this time as he ran into view and skidded to a confused halt in front of the Spartan soldiers.

"Explain!" barked the leader of the soldiers.

"He's a deserter from Thermopylae," said Drakon breathlessly. "The boys too."

"I fought for Sparta, and when you unjustly swore to kill my family, Drakon, I went to protect them as any man would." Adakios couldn't keep the hatred out of his voice. "Did your superior, Aristodamus, not tell you that the helots at Thermopylae were to be left unharmed? Did he not have you whipped for arguing?"

Drakon turned pale with rage. He leapt forward and swung his sword wildly at Adakios, who saw him coming and ducked neatly out of the way.

"Enough!" shouted the Spartan, waving at some of his soldiers. "You three men, keep the helots here tonight and then take them to the barracks tomorrow. If anyone tries to escape, kill him instantly. Drakon, you will come back to Sparta with us tonight. Tomorrow we will let the king decide who is to be punished."

CHAPTER 10

That night did not pass quickly. Finn explained in whispers to a slightly confused Arthur that Sparta always had two kings. So while Leonidas was fighting and dying at Thermopylae, another king remained in Sparta. It sounded as though the king would dispense some kind of military justice the following day. Drakon did not seem to be well liked by any

Spartans they had met, but he was still one of their own, and wasn't it true that the Spartans were always on the lookout for signs of helot disobedience or unrest?

None of them slept: they simply sat, and waited, and worried as the smell of Adakios's burning farm buildings reminded them just how much Drakon wanted them dead. They all hoped that Argos, Kassandra and the others had made good their escape, and mercifully none of the Spartans had asked about other inhabitants from the farm. But their own prospects looked grim.

The soldiers, for their part, took shifts sleeping and guarding their prisoners, and said very little. At dawn they were ordered to their feet, dimly registering the storm clouds that were gathering above them. The soldiers made it very clear that no talking was permitted, and another long trudge began as they followed the river upstream towards Sparta. Other than very brief stops to drink from the river, they kept up a continuous silent march until they reached the outskirts of the city. They marched along wide lanes, between simple white houses with red-tiled roofs, and quickly arrived at a particularly long white wall. Two Spartans stood guarding a double gate in the wall, their bronze armour gleaming even in the gloomy light. The air was heavy beneath the dark clouds. Something was going to burst.

"Mikanos's prisoners," one of the boys' guards barked. They marched through the gates without breaking step, and on across a wide courtyard towards a low, flat-roofed building with a long row of narrow doorways. Without a word they were pushed through one of the doorways. The door was shut behind them and they found themselves alone, blinking to adjust their eyes to the dim light of a small cell.

For a long while none of them spoke. Outside they could hear the clipped commands and stamping feet of soldiers being drilled. Inside, they leaned wearily against the walls of the cell and sank into their thoughts.

"At least your family escaped," said Arthur eventually.

"I hope so," said Adakios, nodding his head slowly. "And I have you to thank for that. But I still don't understand who you are and why you have done so much for me."

This was awkward. *Because in around 2,500 years'*

time your ghost will send us back in time to fix something that went wrong for your family? Finn wished he could say something like that to one of their warriors, just once.

"I suppose we were just in the right place at the right time," he said instead.

"Like Arthur in the cave, with that bear," said Adakios quietly. "But how did he get into the cave in the first place?"

"Look, we can't explain it," said Arthur, "but you know we're here to help you."

"What's going to happen to us now?" said Finn, trying to change the subject.

Adakios frowned and said nothing. The door opened with a sudden thump and the moment had passed. A guard ordered them to their feet and out of the cell, and they stumbled out once more into the courtyard. They were led to a wall, and then through it into a much bigger compound. This was clearly where the soldiers had been practising their drill. Row upon row of fully armed Spartan soldiers stood at attention, their red-plumed helmets swaying in the breeze and their huge spears thrust up to the sky.

In total silence, the Spartans faced a podium at one end of the compound. On it stood two men, one of whom was addressing the soldiers.

"... and it was thus that a mere three hundred of our warriors brought great glory on themselves, and on Sparta, and stood firm against a hundred thousand Persians at Thermopylae, allowing the rest of our armies to retreat."

The guards shoved Adakios and the boys around the perimeter of the compound.

Something was niggling away at the back of Finn's mind, until he saw Drakon standing behind the podium and momentarily forgot about everything else. Though he stood freely and unguarded, Drakon looked... frightened!

"It was Leonidas himself who led the men to their certain deaths," the speaker on the podium went on. "And so Sparta has sacrificed a king as the oracle demanded. He sent me, Aristodamus, to tell the story of the three hundred."

At the mention of Aristodamus Finn jolted. *Of course,* he thought. *I knew I recognised his voice!* Just then, Aristodamus turned to the second man, and Finn caught sight of the speaker's face. There was no doubt – he was the man who had flogged Drakon back at Thermopylae. *Maybe,* thought Finn, *just maybe, there might be a way out of this!* Glancing at Arthur and Adakios he could see that they recognised him too. The second man on the podium stepped forward.

"As Aristodamus has said, Leonidas and those three hundred men have brought great glory on Sparta. I, Leotychidas, will honour their memories as your king, by ensuring that Xerxes and his Persian horde are driven out of these lands forever!"

So this is the other king of Sparta! thought Finn.

"Now, word has reached me of a group of deserters from Thermopylae, rounded up by our men last night. Bring them forward!"

The guards pushed Adakios and the boys to the front of the podium. "Kneel before your king!" someone shouted, and they were forced down. Finn glanced up and caught sight of Aristodamus staring at them in wide-eyed surprise. His eyes narrowed when the king called the ashen-faced Drakon forward.

"These helots deserted the army at Thermopylae, and you captured them?" King Leotychidas asked.

"Yes, great King, they are deserters," said Drakon, looking at the ground.

"There is no defence against a charge of desertion," said the king, his voice cold. "But if you have anything to say you may say it."

Adakios cleared his throat.

This had better be good, thought Finn.

"Great King," Adakios began, "when the call came I was happy to march against the Persians, and in her wisdom Sparta promised me my freedom in return. No longer would my family or I be helots. This I have dreamed of all my life, so you can understand that I would not choose to desert the army, knowing the price that I would pay when I was caught."

"Yet you ran like a rat!" Drakon snarled.

"You swore you would kill my family!" Adakios retorted. "And with no provocation! But I wonder, did you drive my nephew and me to flight so that you would have your own excuse to leave Thermopylae?"

Drakon turned to the king, but the fury on his face turned to despair as Aristodamus stepped forward and spoke quietly. Finn could only make out some of Aristodamus's words, but it was clear that he was telling the king the truth of the story.

The king stood silent for a while, and the only sound in the compound was the faint rustle of the soldiers' plumed helmets.

"Drakon," he said at length, "you disobeyed Aristodamus, your superior, and drove the helots away. Your insubordination would be severely punishable in any case, but that you then pursued the helots and abandoned the army at Thermopylae makes you a deserter as much as they." Drakon's face was stony.

"And you," he said, gesturing to Adakios and the boys, "no matter how he threatened you, you should not have deserted, though I can see that yours was not the first fault." He fell silent again, as Drakon, Adakios, Arthur and Finn all held their breath.

"I do not believe that either of you fled from Thermopylae out of cowardice, but flee you did, and all because of a feud between you. So we will let the gods settle the matter. Drakon, you will fight the helot here, today, to the death. These two boys have thrown in their lot with him, and they shall share his fate." He waved a hand towards Arthur and Finn as he said this. "The winner will have two days to leave the kingdom of Sparta. After that he too will be killed. Guards, arm them! Soldiers, form a theatre!"

Finn looked at Adakios. His eyes burned bright with hope and determination now that a path had opened up that led him back to his family. Drakon, who had begun to tremble at the mention of exile, had regained his composure. However, the hate in his eyes was like nothing Finn had ever seen.

The soldiers had re-formed around the perimeter of the compound, four human walls with a large square in the middle, ready for the duel to begin. Drakon and Adakios stared at each other as the guards prepared them. Armour and helmets were strapped in place. Sword belts were wrapped around waists, and each man was presented with a shield and a long spear. By the time they stepped forward into the open square, they were transformed into Spartan warriors.

They drew lots out of an upturned helmet held by one of the guards to decide who would be first to throw

their spear, and Drakon won this little victory. The two men walked to opposite corners of the square, then turned and waited, glaring at one another.

"Whichever man has angered the gods, let him die and descend to Hades!" cried the king, and the four walls of soldiers echoed his prayer.

At the word 'Hades', Drakon let fly with his spear. It arched across the square and glanced off Adakios's raised shield. Adakios took careful aim and hurled his own spear in turn. Its flight was closer to horizontal and it thudded into Drakon's shield, piercing it and drawing a cry of pain from the Spartan as it tore into his flesh. Drakon stumbled back as Adakios sprinted across the square, sword drawn now, roaring himself on. His sword crashed down on Drakon's helmet and shattered in his hand. A stunned Drakon fell to the floor and Adakios, now weaponless, grabbed the plume of Drakon's helmet and began dragging him across the dirt, throttling him with the leather chinstrap.

Drakon's feet were scrabbling for purchase in the dust as he was dragged along, his hands at his throat, until his chinstrap snapped and the helmet came away in Adakios's hands. The helot threw it into the ranks of soldiers to one side. Drakon had hauled himself unsteadily to his feet and half-drawn his sword, but with another fierce battle cry Adakios leapt on his enemy and knocked him back down. The sword fell loose and clattered to the ground. Adakios, knees on Drakon's chest, reached for the sword and in one fluid movement made the fatal slash across Drakon's neck.

Triumphant, Adakios raised his face to the heavens just as the storm clouds burst and rain poured down in torrents, mixing with Drakon's blood in the dust.

Arthur looked at Finn. "It's over!" he said. "The Crypteia are no threat to his family any longer."

Suddenly the boys both felt too exhausted to stand. They collapsed to the floor as the rain intensified, until they felt as though they were swimming through it. The bronze armour and red plumes of the Spartan warriors began to fade and, as the boys closed their eyes, Sparta slipped away.

BONUS BITS!

What's the point of an introduction?

Introductions in books often set the scene and give the reader vital background information needed to understand the story. This is certainly the case in the story you have just read!

Test your knowledge by saying which of the following statements are TRUE and which are FALSE, based on the information given to you in the introduction to this book.

1. The Hall of Heroes is a museum about warriors throughout history.

2. Finn and Arthur are brothers.

3. The Hall of Heroes is a museum about animals throughout history.

4. The Hall of Heroes is haunted by the ghosts of warriors whose belongings are there.

5. Arthur and Finn have a great grandfather called Professor Spartan.

6. Arthur and Finn have a great grandfather called Professor Blade.

7. Finn wrote down everything the Professor told him in a book called *Warrior Heroes*.

8. Arthur wrote down everything the Professor told him in a book called *Warrior Heroes*.

INTERESTING WORDS
(that Finn doesn't tell you more about!)

There are lots of words related to the ancient Greek world in this story. Here is a short guide to some of the most important ones!

ARES
the Greek (and Roman) god of war

ATHENS
the capital of Greece

GREAVES
armour worn to protect shins

HADES
the Greek (and Roman) god of the underworld and the ruler of the dead

HELOT
a member of a class of serfs from ancient Sparta – in between a slave and a citizen

HIPPODROME
(in ancient Greece) an oval track for horse races and chariot races

OLYMPIA
a place in southern Greece that was the religious centre devoted to the worship of Zeus

PERSIANS
natives or inhabitants of Persia (now known as Iran)

SPARTANS
citizens of Sparta

THERMOPYLAE
a mountain pass near the sea in northern Greece, where several battles took place in ancient times

XERXES
the fourth king of Persia

ZEUS
the supreme god of the ancient Greeks

WHAT NEXT?

If you enjoyed this story, why not find out more information about the Spartans, the Persians or even the battle of Thermopylae? Use books and the internet for your research and then present your work (to your friends or family) using one of the following methods.

· a computer presentation

· a poem

· a poster

· a short role-play (with help from some friends)

· a book (why not dye the paper brown and curl the edges to make it look old?)

Answers to 'What's the point of an introduction?'

1. True
2. True
3. False
4. True
5. False
6. True
7. True
8. False

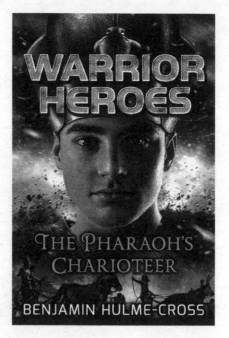

WARRIOR HEROES
The Pharaoh's Charioteer

Benjamin Hulme-Cross

Join Arthur and Finn on another adventure,
as they travel back to ancient Egypt to discover
dangerous rivalries and a prince and princess
with strong opinions. Can they prevent
a kidnapping and stop a war?

£4.99

9781472925893